To Zoe and Lilli— HAPPY READING!

The
ALPHABET
PARADE

by

Charles Ghigna

CHARLES GHIGNA

2002

Illustrated *by* Patti Woods

love you guys—

Patti Woods

RIVER CITY KIDS
1719 Mulberry Street
Montgomery, AL 36106

In memory of
Mali Moore
librarian, artist, friend

RIVER CITY KIDS
1719 Mulberry Street
Montgomery, AL 36106

First Edition

Library of Congress Cataloging-in-Publication Data

Ghigna, Charles.
The alphabet parade / by Charles Ghigna ; illustrated by Patti Woods.
p. cm.
Summary: A parade of animals and people presents the alphabet, from an
acrobat walking on his hands to the zebra with his stripes.
ISBN 1-880216-74-4 (alk. paper)
[1. Parades--Fiction. 2. Animals--Fiction. 3. Alphabet. 4. Stories in
rhymes.] I. Woods, Patti, ill. II. Title.
PZ8.3.G345 Al 2002
[E]--dc21
2001005794

Printed in China

The Alphabet Parade,

Oh what a sight to see!

A band of marching letters

All the way from A to Z!

Acrobat

A is for the

who
marches
on
his
hands.

B

B

B e a r

B

is for the
baby

who
bangs a
pair of
pans.

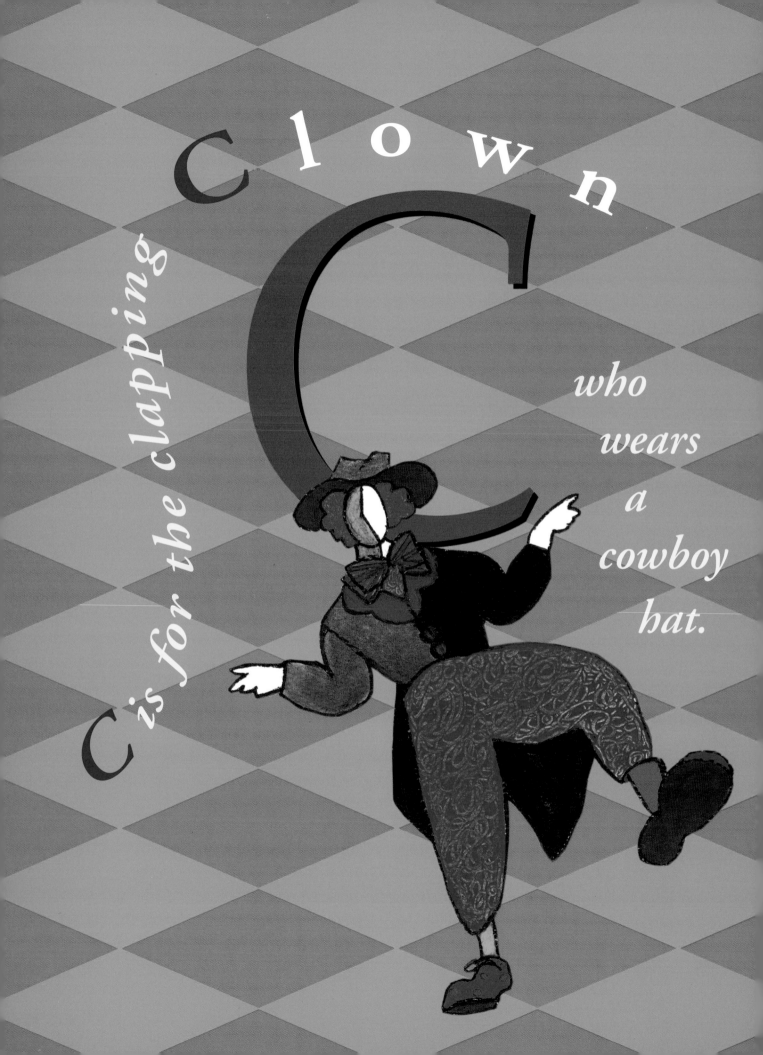

C l o w n

C is for the clapping

who
wears
a
cowboy
hat.

D

is for the

dancing

D o g

D

who

dances

with a

cat.

E is for the Elephant

who
waves
at
everyone.

F

is for the
friendly

F o x

F

who
fiddles
just
for fun.

G
is for the
young
Giraffe

who
gallops
past the
crowd.

Hippo

H is for the

who
hollers
right
out
loud.

I

is for the

I b i s

I

who
rides
upon a
float.

J

J **a** **g** **u** **a** **r**

J is for the

who

jumps

a

giant

rope.

K is for the **Kinkajou**

who ties his tail in knots.

L

is for the

Leopard

L

who
likes to
count
his
spots.

M
is for the
M o n k e y

who
marches
with
his
toys.

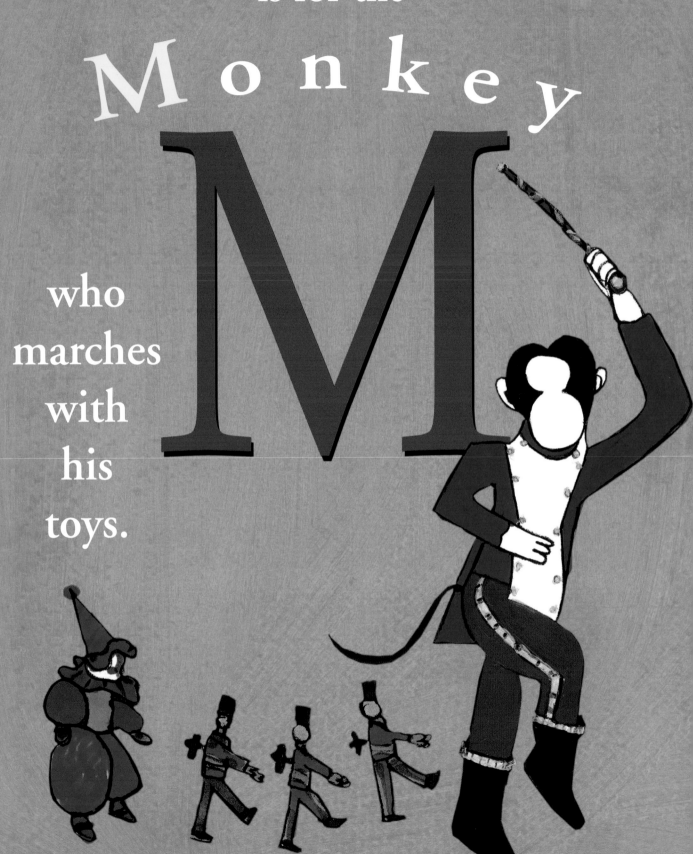

N is for the N**ewt**

who
wears
his
corduroys.

O

is for the

O s t r i c h

and
his
orange
underwear.

Panda

P

P is for the

and
his friend
the
polar
bear.

Q

is for the royal

Queen

Q

who
leads a
quacking
duck.

R is for the **Rhino**

who drives a pickup truck.

S e a l

S

S is for the slippery

who
splashes
in
his tub.

Tiger

T is for the

and
her
tiny
tiger cub.

U
nicorn
U is for the

who
pulls a
mighty
urn.

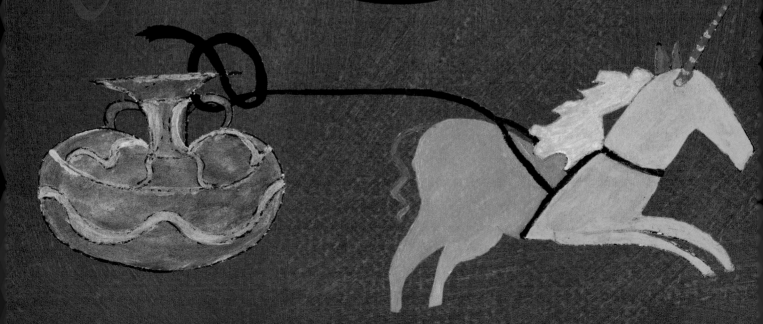

V

is for the

Vulture

V

who's
talking
to the
tern.

W
is for the
W o l f
W

and
the
wallaby.

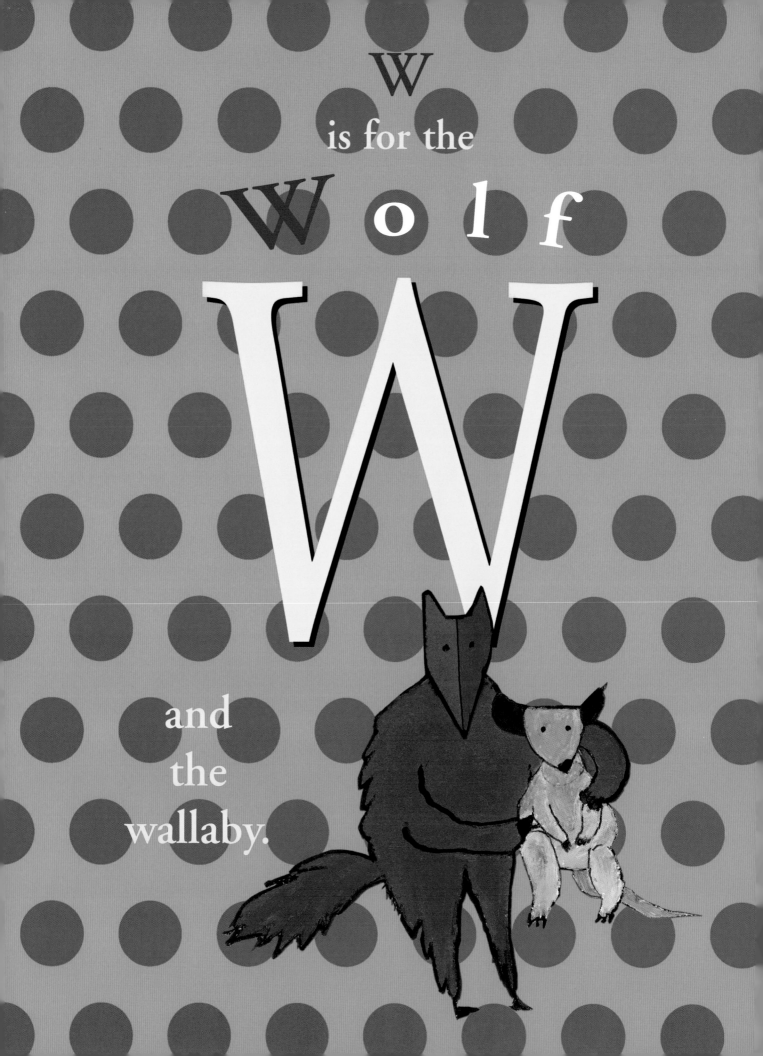

X is for the **X**ylophone

they
play
while
sipping
tea!

Y
is for the

Y

Yellow hair

upon
the
hairy
yak.

Z is for the
Zebra

z e b r a

Z

with the
stripes
upon
his
back.

And so we say good-bye today
To all the friends we made,
To all the marching letters in

The
Alphabet
Parade!

CHARLES GHIGNA (aka Father Goose)
is the author of more than thirty books of poetry for
children and adults. His most recent titles include
*Animal Trunk: Silly Poems to Read Aloud, One Hundred
Shoes, See The Yak Yak,* and *Mice Are Nice.* For more
information, please visit the Father Goose website
at www.CharlesGhigna.com

PATTI WOODS
is a graphic artist and designer, as well as a fine artist
whose works appear in galleries and private collections.
Her artworks and designs have appeared on CD covers,
books and magazines. This is her first children's book.